ATOMIC BOMB PERSPECTIVES

HOW THE BOMB
CHANGED
EVERYTHING

BY EMMA HUDDLESTON

CONTENT CONSULTANT
Allan M. Winkler
University Distinguished Professor of History (Emeritus)
Miami University of Ohio

Core Library

An Imprint of Abdo Publishing
abdobooks.com

Cover image: People protest nuclear weapons development in 1959
on the anniversary of the Hiroshima bombing.

abdobooks.com

Published by Abdo Publishing, a division of ABDO, PO Box 398166, Minneapolis, Minnesota 55439. Copyright © 2022 by Abdo Consulting Group, Inc. International copyrights reserved in all countries. No part of this book may be reproduced in any form without written permission from the publisher. Core Library™ is a trademark and logo of Abdo Publishing.

Printed in the United States of America, North Mankato, Minnesota
052021
092021

THIS BOOK CONTAINS
RECYCLED MATERIALS

Cover Photo: Bettmann/Getty Images
Interior Photos: Universal History Archive/Universal Images Group/Getty Images, 4–5; Los Alamos National Laboratory/The LIFE Picture Collection/Getty Images, 7; AP Images, 12–13, 25, 45; Album/Fine Art Images/Newscom, 15, 43; Everett Collection/Newscom, 18–19; Pallava Bagla/Corbis News/Getty Images, 21; Vladimir Samokhotsky/TASS/Getty Images, 28–29; Red Line Editorial, 30, 40; Rena Schild/Shutterstock Images, 36–37

Editor: Maddie Spalding
Series Designer: Ryan Gale

Library of Congress Control Number: 2019954296

Publisher's Cataloging-in-Publication Data

Names: Huddleston, Emma, author
Title: How the bomb changed everything / by Emma Huddleston
Description: Minneapolis, Minnesota : Abdo Publishing, 2022 | Series: Atomic bomb perspectives | Includes online resources and index
Identifiers: ISBN 9781532192678 (lib. bdg.) | ISBN 9781098210571 (ebook)
Subjects: LCSH: Nuclear warfare--Juvenile literature. | Weapons of mass destruction--Juvenile literature. | Nuclear weapons control--Juvenile literature. | Nuclear weapons--Safety measures--Juvenile literature.
Classification: DDC 940.5401--dc23

CONTENTS

CHAPTER ONE
A Turning Point **4**

CHAPTER TWO
The Cold War **12**

CHAPTER THREE
Nuclear Development **18**

CHAPTER FOUR
The Effects of Radiation **28**

CHAPTER FIVE
Today's Nuclear Issues **36**

Important Dates **42**

Stop and Think **44**

Glossary **46**

Online Resources **47**

Learn More **47**

Index **48**

About the Author **48**

A TURNING POINT

O n August 14, 1945, people across the United States waved newspapers in the air. They rejoiced. The papers shared important news. Earlier that day, Japan had agreed to stop fighting the United States and its allies. Japanese officials made this decision after the United States dropped two atomic bombs on Japan.

Japan officially surrendered a few weeks later. Japanese and US officials met on a US Navy battleship on September 2.

Americans celebrated Japan's surrender on August 14, 1945. Newspapers used the offensive term *Jap* to talk about the Japanese people.

Japanese leaders signed the terms of surrender. Japan's surrender ended World War II (1939–1945).

The United States had been on the side of the Allies during the war. The other main Allied countries were France, Great Britain, and the Soviet Union. The Allies fought against Germany, Italy, and Japan. These countries made up the Axis powers.

The war had broken out when German troops invaded Poland in 1939. The United States entered the war on December 8, 1941, by declaring war against Japan. Japan had attacked a US military base one day earlier. The military base was in Pearl Harbor, Hawaii. Japanese planes had bombed the base, killing more than 2,400 Americans.

SURPRISE ATTACKS

On May 7, 1945, Germany surrendered. But the war was not over. Japan continued to fight the Allies.

US scientists pull radioactive material from a shed in January 1944. The top-secret project to build an atomic bomb was called the Manhattan Project.

The United States had developed an atomic bomb. US officials decided to use it against Japan.

On the morning of August 6, 1945, the United States dropped an atomic bomb over Hiroshima in Japan. The bomb destroyed approximately 4 square miles (11 sq km) of the city. Approximately 80,000 people were instantly killed. The atomic bomb was the most powerful weapon the world had ever seen.

US officials expected Japan to surrender immediately after the bombing. They waited just a few days. They heard nothing from Japanese leaders. So the United States decided to drop another atomic bomb on Japan. On August 9, the United States dropped this bomb over the city of Nagasaki. The blast instantly killed approximately 40,000 people. About one month later, Japan officially surrendered.

Both bombings left lingering problems for decades. The bombs released radiation when they exploded.

Radiation is a powerful and harmful type of energy. It continued to be released into the environment after the explosion. It caused illnesses, including radiation sickness and cancer. Many people died from these illnesses. Others died from severe burn injuries. No one can be sure of the exact death toll. Experts estimate that 210,000 people died in Hiroshima and Nagasaki within a year as a result of the bombings.

LITTLE BOY AND FAT MAN

The nicknames of the atomic bombs were Little Boy and Fat Man. The United States dropped Little Boy on Hiroshima. It weighed 9,700 pounds (4,400 kg). The United States dropped Fat Man on Nagasaki. Fat Man weighed 10,800 pounds (5,000 kg). Little Boy contained the element uranium. Fat Man was made of plutonium. Uranium and plutonium atoms were split inside the bombs. This released a lot of energy.

THE FIRST ATOMIC BOMBS

The bombs the United States had developed were the first atomic weapons used in warfare. An atomic bomb is a powerful weapon. Its explosion is caused by reactions in the bomb's core. The core is the center of the bomb. The reactions happen when atoms break apart. Atoms are bound together by a strong force. They release an enormous amount of energy and heat when they are split.

Many US officials believed the atomic bomb was the only option that would quickly end World War II. However, people disagree about whether dropping the bomb was necessary. Some think the war would have ended around the same time without the bombs. Others believe the war would have dragged on longer. They think the bombs brought an early end to the war.

The atomic bombs showed scientific advancement. They were a sign of military and political power. The US military had the biggest weapon in the world. But it would not be the only country with nuclear weapons for long.

EXPLORE ONLINE

Chapter One describes the US bombing of Hiroshima. The website below goes into more depth on this topic. As you know, every source is different. How is the information from the website the same as the information in Chapter One? What new information did you learn?

THE ATOMIC BOMBING OF HIROSHIMA

abdocorelibrary.com/bomb-changed-everything

THE COLD WAR

During World War II, the United States and the Soviet Union were allies. But their relationship was tense. After the war ended, these tensions remained. The United States and Soviet Union entered a period known as the Cold War (1947–1991).

The Cold War was unlike most wars. Soldiers did not fight each other. Each country tried to show its power in other ways. Both competed to make bigger and better nuclear weapons. This competition

During the Cold War, the Soviet Union held a parade each year on May 1. It displayed its military weapons.

13

SPIES FOR THE SOVIET UNION

Julius and Ethel Rosenberg were US citizens. They organized a spy ring for the Soviet Union. They lived in New York City. Atomic scientist Klaus Fuchs was part of their spy ring. The spies gathered information about how the United States built its weapons. They shared this information with the Soviet Union. Some historians believe Fuchs's efforts helped Soviet scientists create an atomic bomb a few years earlier than they would have on their own. Fuchs and the Rosenbergs were later uncovered as spies. Fuchs was arrested in 1950. He spent nine years in prison. The Rosenbergs were executed in 1953.

was known as the arms race.

Each country tried to figure out its enemy's plans. Both sides used spies to gather information. Spies learned about military plans, weapon development, and more.

On August 29, 1949, the Soviet Union tested its first atomic bomb. The bomb was similar to the bomb dropped on

The Soviet Union conducted many nuclear weapons tests at Semipalatinsk, a site in Kazakhstan.

Nagasaki, called Fat Man. Its core was made of plutonium.

THE H-BOMB

In the late 1940s, US scientists started development on a new type of weapon. US officials wanted to create the most powerful weapon in the world. It was called a hydrogen bomb, or an H-bomb. H-bombs are more powerful than atomic bombs. They contain hydrogen. They also contain plutonium or uranium. In an H-bomb, an atomic reaction detonates the hydrogen. This process releases a lot of energy.

The first US test of an H-bomb happened in 1952. Scientists detonated the bomb at Eniwetok Atoll. This is an island in the South Pacific. The bomb's blast was nearly 1,000 times stronger than the bomb the United States dropped on Hiroshima. The H-bomb's success put the United States ahead in the arms race. In response, the Soviet Union developed its own H-bomb. The Soviets tested this bomb in 1953. It was not as powerful as the H-bomb developed by the United States.

PERSPECTIVES

ADVISING THE PRESIDENT

In 1949, the General Advisory Committee wrote a report for US president Harry S. Truman. The committee was made up of scientists. Robert Oppenheimer was the group's leader. Oppenheimer had led the effort to build the atomic bombs that were used on Japan. The scientists recommended that Truman end H-bomb development. The report said, "The fact that no limits exist to the destructiveness of this weapon makes its very existence . . . a danger to humanity as a whole. It is necessarily an evil thing considered in any light."

In the 1960s, the threat of war escalated. The Soviet Union set up missiles in Cuba. The Soviets aimed these missiles at the United States. US officials found out about these missiles. This led to greater tensions between the two countries. The tensions almost led to war. But the Soviets never attacked. The two countries came to an agreement. The Soviets removed the missiles from Cuba. In exchange, US officials promised not to invade Cuba. This standoff was called the Cuban Missile Crisis.

FURTHER EVIDENCE

Chapter Two has quite a bit of information about the Cold War. Identify one of the chapter's main points. What evidence does the author provide to support this point? Read the article at the website below. Does the information on the website support the point you identified? Does it present new evidence?

WHAT WAS THE COLD WAR?

abdocorelibrary.com/bomb-changed-everything

NUCLEAR DEVELOPMENT

I n 1953, US president Dwight D. Eisenhower made a speech. His speech was called "Atoms for Peace." He encouraged scientists to focus on ways people could benefit from nuclear power. Nuclear power could have nonmilitary purposes. It could generate electricity and be used as a source of energy.

Eisenhower created a program to share scientific knowledge with other countries. The countries could use this knowledge to

President Dwight D. Eisenhower, *left*, *seated*, signed the Atomic Energy Act of 1954. The act helped develop US nuclear power programs.

develop nuclear power. In exchange, the countries were supposed to promise to not make nuclear weapons. But countries such as India and Pakistan used this information to make nuclear weapons in the 1960s and 1970s.

DANGEROUS WASTE

Nuclear energy is cheaper to develop than traditional power sources. These sources include fossil fuels such as coal, oil, and gas. Fossil fuels are expensive to buy and burn. Nuclear energy uses water and uranium, which are more affordable.

Additionally, burning fossil fuels releases carbon dioxide and other gases. These gases are called greenhouse gases. They trap heat in Earth's atmosphere. Too much of these gases causes global temperatures to rise. Nuclear power is an alternative energy source. In a nuclear power plant, uranium atoms are split in a reactor. This releases energy as heat. The heat turns water into steam. The steam

The Obninsk Nuclear Power Plant was in operation for 48 years. The plant's control center was preserved and can be seen in Russia today.

powers a machine that is connected to a generator. The generator produces electricity. This process does not release greenhouse gases. Many people promoted nuclear power for this reason.

The first working nuclear power plant was built in Obninsk, the Soviet Union, in 1954. Within four years, England and the United States also had nuclear power plants. These power plants did not create the pollution that traditional power plants do. But they did create nuclear waste. This material is radioactive. This means that it releases harmful energy. This energy can pollute the land and air. It can harm living things.

Some parts of nuclear power plants need to be replaced every few years. People try to dispose of these parts and the nuclear waste in a safe way. Objects remain radioactive for hundreds of years. They must be stored carefully to avoid harming the

POLLUTING THE OCEAN

From 1946 to 1993, many countries dumped nuclear waste in the ocean. They also buried the waste under the ocean floor. This disposal method kept the waste away from where people lived. Laws in Europe said the waste had to be more than 2.5 miles (4 km) below the ocean's surface. The waste also had to be far away from coasts. But some ship captains disregarded these laws. They dumped the waste close to shore. In 1993, international laws were passed that made it illegal to dump radioactive waste in oceans.

environment. Some people buried parts of nuclear power plants in concrete.

In the United States, people buried nuclear waste deep in the ground. However, some of this waste was dumped in the ocean. The United States and 12 other countries disposed of some waste in this way. From 1950 to 1963, European countries dumped 28,500 containers of nuclear waste into the English Channel. Waste leaked out of the containers and harmed animals and other living things. Some radioactive material still remains in the area today.

SPEAKING OUT

Many people thought nuclear power plants were not worth the risk. Nuclear waste was not the only issue. People worried that the core could overheat. The core is where the nuclear reactions take place. If the core were to overheat, the reactor would release radioactive matter. People could die. This type of accident is called a meltdown.

THE THREE MILE ISLAND ACCIDENT

On March 28, 1979, an accident happened at a nuclear power plant in Pennsylvania. The plant was called Three Mile Island. A problem happened in one of the plant's nuclear reactors. In a reactor, a system is supposed to move heat away from the core. This system stopped working. The reactor melted. Some radioactive gas was released. Officials evacuated people from the area. No one died or was injured. But the accident prompted people to create better safety controls at nuclear power plants.

An antinuclear movement developed after the US atomic bomb attacks in Japan. This movement grew after nuclear power plants became widespread. Antinuclear activists were against nuclear development. They thought nuclear weapons were unnecessary and too destructive. Activists also believed nuclear power plants were too dangerous.

In 1955, the first World Conference

Antinuclear protests and demonstrations were common in the 1960s, especially in large cities such as New York City.

Against Atomic and Hydrogen Bombs was held in Hiroshima. People spoke out against nuclear weapons testing. They worried about the effects of radiation.

They feared that nuclear warfare could break out at any time.

Some people built bomb shelters in their backyards. Schools held drills to teach students what to do in the event of a nuclear attack. Students learned to drop to the ground. They practiced crawling under their desks and covering their heads.

TREATIES

The antinuclear movement made more people aware of the dangers of nuclear development. It influenced some government officials. In 1963, the first Nuclear Test-Ban Treaty was written. Officials from the United States, the Soviet Union, and the United Kingdom signed this document. The treaty banned nuclear weapons testing above ground and in the atmosphere. But underground testing continued. Five years later, the Treaty on the Non-Proliferation of Nuclear Weapons was created. The same three countries signed this treaty. They agreed to not help other countries develop nuclear weapons.

STRAIGHT TO THE
SOURCE

Yoshiro Yamawaki lived in Nagasaki at the time of the bombing. He was 11 years old when the attack happened. He became a part of the antinuclear movement. He said:

> *Nuclear weapons should, under no circumstances, be used against humans. However, nuclear powers such as the US and Russia own stockpiles of well over 15,000 nuclear weapons. Not only that, technological advances have given way to a new kind of bomb that can deliver a blast over 1,000 times that of the Hiroshima bombing.*
>
> *Weapons of this capacity must be abolished from the earth. . . . I pray that younger generations will come together to work toward a world free of nuclear weapons.*

Source: Haruka Sakaguchi. "Mr. Yoshiro Yamawaki." *1945 Project*, 2019, 1945project.com. Accessed 16 Jan. 2020.

CHANGING MINDS

In this passage, Yamawaki explains why he thinks nuclear weapons should be banned. Take a position on this issue. Imagine that your best friend has the opposite opinion. Write a short essay to try to change your friend's mind. Make sure you explain your opinion. Include facts and details that support your reasons.

THE EFFECTS OF RADIATION

O n April 28, 1986, workers at a nuclear power plant in Sweden set off alarms. Machines in the plant had detected high levels of radiation on the workers. The workers reported the warnings to their bosses. The bosses told Swedish officials about the high radiation levels. Authorities traced the radiation to the Chernobyl nuclear power plant. This plant was in the city of Pripyat in what is now Ukraine. An accident had happened at Chernobyl two days earlier.

The Chernobyl nuclear power plant opened in 1977. There were four nuclear reactors in the plant.

MAJOR NUCLEAR
ACCIDENTS

Many nuclear-related accidents have happened since the 1950s. This chart gives details about some of these accidents. What new information did you learn from this chart? Did anything surprise you?

DATE	LOCATION	EFFECTS
September 29, 1957	Kyshtym nuclear plant in the Soviet Union	More than 10,000 people were evacuated, and hundreds died.
January 3, 1961	Idaho National Laboratory, Idaho	An explosion in a nuclear reactor killed three people.
March 28, 1979	Three Mile Island nuclear power station near Harrisburg, Pennsylvania	A partial nuclear meltdown released small amounts of radiation. There were no resulting deaths or illnesses.
April 26, 1986	Chernobyl nuclear power plant in Pripyat, present-day Ukraine	Radiation poisoning killed around 30 people during the first three months after a reactor explosion.
September 30, 1999	Conversion Test Building in Tokaimura, Japan	Two workers died, and hundreds were exposed to high levels of radiation.
March 11, 2011	Fukushima Daiichi nuclear plant in Japan	The plant's cooling systems failed after a tsunami, which caused explosions. More than 100,000 people were evacuated.

The Chernobyl disaster happened when a reactor exploded during a safety test. The blast made the roof fly off. Radioactive debris flew out. Walls collapsed. The heat of the explosion started fires. Nearby buildings, trees, and other objects caught fire or melted. The core continued to burn for days.

Wind carried the debris all around the world. The debris was not visible. It covered the Swedish workers and other people in neighboring countries. The debris had set off the alarms at the Swedish power plant.

Soviet officials tried to cover up the accident. They did not warn people about the danger of exposure. Radiation poisoning from the explosion killed 31 people. Of those, 28 were power plant workers and firefighters who helped during the meltdown.

LONG-TERM DAMAGE

The Chernobyl disaster created widespread concern about nuclear power. It was an example of what could go wrong in a nuclear power plant. The effects of the

PERSPECTIVES

AN EMPTY CITY

Robert Peter Gale went to the Soviet Union after the Chernobyl disaster. Gale was a US doctor. He treated people who had radiation sickness. He performed 19 surgeries. Only five of his patients survived. On a second trip back to the Soviet Union, he flew in a helicopter to see the city where the explosion had happened. He remembered, "We kept circling and circling, but none of us could really speak. I had a strong feeling we were seeing history that I hoped we'd never see again. . . . I could not take my eyes off the scene."

explosion were long-lasting.

The radioactive debris polluted the land, water, and air. It contaminated plants. It also contaminated livestock, fish, and other animals. Some of these animals died from radiation sickness.

The Chernobyl disaster affected the survivors too. Those who had lived in Pripyat were forced to relocate. Everyone who lived within 18 miles (30 km) of the plant had to move. Some people were burned or injured from the explosion. Cancer, blindness, and radiation sickness were common among survivors. Many died or suffered from these ailments.

THE END OF NUCLEAR TESTING

The Soviet Union began to break apart in 1989. Soviet leader Mikhail Gorbachev stepped down in 1991. The Cold War ended. Russia was one of the countries created from the former Soviet Union. It took over the Soviet Union's nuclear weapons. The United States and Russia signed the Strategic Arms Reduction Treaty. They agreed to reduce the number of nuclear weapons in their stockpiles.

On September 23, 1992, the last US nuclear weapon test happened in Nevada. On October 2, President George H. W. Bush announced the end of US nuclear testing. The country had performed 1,054 nuclear weapons tests in 47 years.

The United States and Russia had been leaders in nuclear development. As nuclear development slowed

THE NEVADA TEST SITE

US scientists tested nuclear weapons at the Nevada Test Site (NTS) from 1951 to 1992. This site is 65 miles (105 km) north of Las Vegas, Nevada. Some tests happened above ground. Scientists also conducted underground tests. The NTS was renamed the Nevada National Security Site (NNSS) in 2010. Today, scientists at the NNSS test the groundwater and environment to monitor the radiation levels. Some scientists at the NNSS research nuclear energy. The Department of Homeland Security does training at this site. It prepares plans in case of a nuclear emergency.

in these countries, other countries followed suit. Scientists focused on how to manage stockpiles and safely use nuclear power.

In 1996, more than 180 nations signed the Comprehensive Nuclear-Test-Ban Treaty. The goal of the treaty was to ban nuclear testing worldwide. As of 2020, eight countries still had to agree to the treaty before it could go into effect. The United States was among these countries.

STRAIGHT TO THE
SOURCE

Sergey Krasilnikov was one of more than 800,000 liquidators. These workers cleaned up the surrounding land after the Chernobyl disaster. Krasilnikov helped evacuate people. He discussed his experience in a 2016 interview. He said:

> *In 1994, I got sick. After my medical assessment they said my stroke and paralysis were a direct result of my work as a liquidator. . . .*
>
> *Knowing what I know now, I would probably act in a similar way. . . . I was saving the ordinary people of this country. I was protecting the people of Ukraine from the spreading of nuclear poison. . . . I wish I had lived a different life, but I would not live the one I was given differently.*

Source: Kim Hjelmgaard. "The 'Liquidator': He Cleaned Up After Chernobyl—And Is Paying the Price." *USA Today*, 23 April 2016, usatoday.com. Accessed 16 Jan. 2020.

WHAT'S THE BIG IDEA?

Take a closer look at this passage. What point is the speaker trying to make? What is his perspective on the disaster?

15000 NUKES ≠ SECURITY
#ELIMINATENUKES
NSS leaders put nukes
15,000 nukes ≠ Security!
NUKES
GLOBAL LEADERS be a hero - take a stand DEMAND ZERO
15,000 NUKES ≠ SECURITY
GLOBAL ZERO
15,000 NUKES ≠ SECURITY
globalzero.org #NSS2016

CHAPTER FIVE

TODAY'S NUCLEAR ISSUES

T oday, the antinuclear movement remains strong. Many people protest nuclear development. They ask for laws to ban nuclear weapons and power plants. Debates continue about whether nuclear development is necessary or moral. Nuclear power plant disasters have fueled these debates.

In March 2011, an earthquake and tsunami hit Fukushima, Japan. The power went out at a nuclear power plant. The plant's cooling

Some activist groups, such as Global Zero, advocate for the worldwide elimination of nuclear weapons.

PERSPECTIVES

WHO IS RESPONSIBLE?

The Tokyo Electric Power Company (TEPCO) owned the Fukushima nuclear power plant. Some people thought TEPCO was responsible for the nuclear disaster. They challenged TEPCO in court. They said the company should have prepared more against the tsunami. TEPCO argued that it did not break any safety laws. The court ruled that TEPCO was not guilty. This ruling upset many people. Masakatsu Kanno lived in Fukushima during the disaster. He and his father had to evacuate. His father had been in a hospital. He died after he was evacuated. Kanno said, "It was TEPCO that caused the accident, there is no mistake about it."

systems failed. The reactor cores overheated. Some parts of the machines melted. Holes in the machines leaked heat and radiation, which caused explosions. More than 100,000 people were evacuated from the area. However, officials did not announce that a meltdown had happened. Some people wondered if they were trying to cover up how bad the accident was.

Japanese officials worked for months to stop radiation from spreading. One way they did this was by cooling the building and power plant machines with water. In December, they announced that the disaster was controlled. They found that the radiation had been reduced to a minimal level.

Nuclear power plant accidents often cause a lot of concern. Some people also worry about the effects of living near one of these plants. People who live near these plants could be exposed to a small amount of radiation over a long period of time.

CONTINUED THREATS

As of 2020, North Korea is the only country known to still be testing nuclear weapons. The country is serious about building up its stockpile. North Korean scientists claimed that one of its tests involved a hydrogen bomb. North Korea also has a powerful missile. Many people think this missile would be able to hit the United States.

NUCLEAR WEAPONS STOCKPILES

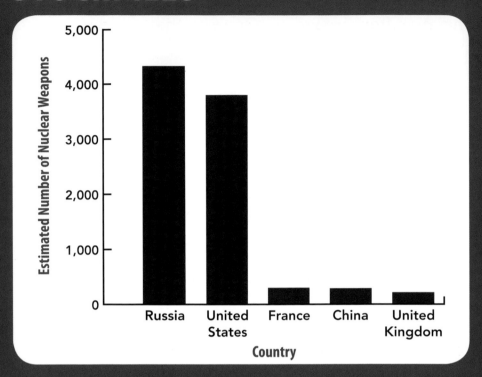

This graph shows the countries with the most nuclear weapons as of 2019. Do you think any country should be able to stockpile nuclear weapons? Why or why not?

These nuclear threats have strained the relationship between the two countries.

As of 2019, nine countries had a total of nearly 14,000 nuclear weapons. Of these, 92 percent belonged to the United States and Russia. Many people worry that a nuclear attack could happen if tensions rise.

While the Hiroshima and Nagasaki bombings happened in the past, nuclear weapons still exist in the world today. People are still searching for a way to regulate nuclear weapons. Additionally, some people think nuclear power should no longer be used as an energy source. History has shown that there are both benefits and risks to nuclear development.

NUCLEAR POWER AND CLIMATE CHANGE

In 2019, nuclear power plants generated 10 percent of the world's electricity. These power plants do not release greenhouse gases. For this reason, some experts think nuclear power is necessary to help fight climate change. By relying on nuclear power, countries could lower the amount of greenhouse gases in the air. This could make the future consequences of climate change less severe. But the process of creating nuclear energy is not totally clean. Machines have to mine uranium. These machines are powered by fossil fuels.

IMPORTANT DATES

August 1945
The United States drops an atomic bomb on Hiroshima, Japan, on August 6. It drops another atomic bomb on Nagasaki three days later.

September 2, 1945
Japan officially surrenders, ending World War II.

1952
The United States tests the world's first hydrogen bomb.

1963
The United States, the United Kingdom, and the Soviet Union sign the Nuclear Test-Ban Treaty.

April 26, 1986
An explosion happens at the Chernobyl nuclear power plant near Pripyat, in the former Soviet Union.

October 2, 1992
President George H. W. Bush declares an end to all
US nuclear weapons testing.

1996
Many countries sign the Comprehensive
Nuclear-Test-Ban Treaty.

March 2011
An earthquake and tsunami cause an accident at a nuclear
power plant in Fukushima, Japan.

STOP AND
THINK

Dig Deeper

After reading this book, what questions do you still have about nuclear development? With an adult's help, find a few reliable sources that can help you answer your questions. Write a paragraph about what you learned.

Surprise Me

Chapter Two discusses how the development of the atomic bombs led to the Cold War. After reading this book, what two or three facts about the bombs' effects did you find most surprising? Write a few sentences about each fact. Why did you find each fact surprising?

Take a Stand

Chapter Three describes the antinuclear movement. It protested nuclear development for years. Do you support nuclear power or nuclear weapons? Do you think the world would be better off without one or both? Explain why in a few sentences.

You Are There

Chapter Four discusses the Chernobyl power plant disaster. Imagine you were in Pripyat after the explosion. Write a letter home telling your family and friends about what you see. Be sure to add plenty of details to your letter.

GLOSSARY

ally
a country or nation that offers support during a time of war

atom
the small particle that makes up a substance

detonate
to cause something to explode

element
a substance with unique properties that is made up of only one type of atom

moral
good and honorable

radiation
dangerous energy released from a nuclear reaction

reactor
a device in a power plant that converts heat into electricity

stockpile
a store of weapons

treaty
a written agreement between two or more countries

tsunami
large, destructive waves caused by an earthquake

ONLINE RESOURCES

To learn more about how the atomic bomb changed everything, visit our free resource websites below.

Visit **abdocorelibrary.com** or scan this QR code for free Common Core resources for teachers and students, including vetted activities, multimedia, and booklinks, for deeper subject comprehension.

Visit **abdobooklinks.com** or scan this QR code for free additional online weblinks for further learning. These links are routinely monitored and updated to provide the most current information available.

LEARN MORE

London, Martha. *Atomic Bomb Survivor Stories*. Abdo Publishing, 2022.

Marquardt, Meg. *Nuclear Energy*. Abdo Publishing, 2017.

INDEX

antinuclear movement, 24–26, 27, 37

Atoms for Peace, 19

Chernobyl, 29–32, 35

Cold War, the, 13–15, 17, 33

Comprehensive Nuclear-Test-Ban Treaty, 34

Cuban Missile Crisis, 17

hydrogen bomb, 15–16, 25, 39

Japan, 5–8, 16, 24, 30, 37, 39

meltdowns, 23, 30, 31, 38

North Korea, 39

nuclear power, 19–24, 29–31, 34, 37–39, 41

nuclear reactors, 20, 23, 24, 30, 31, 38

Nuclear Test-Ban Treaty, 26

nuclear waste, 22–23

plutonium, 9, 15

pollution, 21–22, 32

radiation, 8–9, 25, 29–33, 34, 38–39

Russia, 27, 33, 40

Soviet Union, the, 6, 13–14, 16–17, 21, 26, 30, 31–33

stockpiles, 27, 33–34, 39, 40

Strategic Arms Reduction Treaty, 33

Treaty on the Non-Proliferation of Nuclear Weapons, 26

tsunami, 30, 37, 38

uranium, 9, 15, 20, 41

World War II, 6, 10, 13

About the Author

Emma Huddleston lives in the Twin Cities with her husband. She enjoys writing children's books, and she likes to stay active outside. She thinks learning about the atomic bombs is interesting and important.